MY STONE IS NOT DEAD

ALSO BY PIOTR GAWELKO

"The City of Missing People"

PIOTR ZBIGNIEW GAWELKO

MY
STONE
IS
NOT
DEAD

STANDBY&GO

Copyright 2019 by Piotr Zbigniew Gawelko.

All rights reserved. Except for brief passages quoted in a newspaper, magazine, radio, or television review, no part of this book may be reproduced in any form or by any means, electronic or mechanical, including photographing and recording, or by any information storage and retrieval, without permission in writing from the Publisher.

Manufactured in United States of America

ISBN: 979-8-630345-01-1

CONTENTS

THOUGHTS OF A BIRD – SLAM	1
PUPPET IN THE CAGE	2
SPECTATOR	5
9 LIVES	6
CONTOURS 1	8
LABORATORY	9
THE GRAIN	10
BLACK MADONNA	11
YESTERDAY IN PROVINCETOWN	12
MEANING	14
NEXT	15
KING OF COLORS	16
IF THE WORLD HAS STOPPED TODAY	17
NO TITLE LESS SENSE	18
TERROR	19
LA MAMA E.T.C.	21
OUTFLOW	26
I KNOW	27
OUTRAGEOUS BOYS	29
I WANT TO WRITE ABOUT, AND ONLY	30
AN AD	32
START NEW	34
CONTOURS 2	36
I AM LEAVING	37

UNKNOWN MAN FROM A PAINTING	**39**
BUREAU OF FOUND THINGS	**41**
?	**42**
PHOTO SHOOT	**43**
BLOOD FLOW	**45**
AUSCHWITZ 1	**46**
MY MORNING IN ALUMINIUM SINK	**49**
TO USAIN BOLT	**51**
THE CHOICE	**52**
IN MY FATHER'S HOUSE	**53**
THE WORST POEM I EVER WROTE	**54**
THE REFUGEE	**55**
BLINK	**57**
CAVITATE DEI	**58**
10Q	**59**
POETS ON THE BEACH	**60**
ADDENDA:	
1. THOUGHTS OF A BIRD – SLAM	**65**
Polish version	
2. AUSCHWITZ 1 : Note	**66**

TO NOBODY

THOUGHTS OF A BIRD – SLAM

After the house gains dark again...Am I?

It always comes back for me...dispersing
the gloom
precisely,
so

As easily as I am distracted,
how silently I keep forgetting...Forgive me,
Master Door.
Sun.
I am your testimony.
I fear nothing.

PUPPET IN THE CAGE

1.
I was never to be
born.
the fact I am torn
inside, I don't recall.
at all?

2
papered, metallic, wooden,
upholstered,
heart – erupting,
unstoppable slush ramping my desires,
through my strings, my chains, my wires,
far back breaks down, straight into
my powerlessness.

3.
sewn, glued, patched, screwed body
doesn't have instinct of defense;
chop off my leg, I won't even budge.

4.
although I am scared, you won't see
panic in my
plastic, glass, stuffed, painted, eyes,
no curtain overshadows me,
no man can grasp my sight.

5.
sometimes, I think, He is not fair.
I saw Him over a pond, painting autumn gold;
when questioned, replied
that He loves me,
that He loves me just like the real boys,
who are all beautiful.

6.
where should I keep it, what should I do with
it,
where should I keep it?
my exhausted, thirsty, sidelined, rebellious,
twitching on a web, hope.

7.
somebody better lock me in a cage,
so, me, body,
somebody,
better lock me on *Amen,*
because I am furious
because I am one step away from,
and understand

what's outside the cage.
if I could only hear...
nothing, but nothing would be the same,
nothing, and not least,
last year's snow.

8.
familiar hand is grabbing me;
"yes it's me". I hear.
next I am placed on black square,
on a slanted bench, awaiting, expecting
extraordinariness,
but see instead:
curious, intrigued, laughing, nervous, bored,
moved
people.

one of them, cannot take his eyes off me,
yes,
the boy...that is me
but I could not know.

SPECTATOR

The man is sleeping.
Yes,
he looks pretty in shadow.
Yes,
He moves his leg.

I will bet you a handful of salt
he thinks he is going somewhere.
I will bet you an everything and a nothing.
I will bet you an everything and nothing,
he has one of those fantasies where
dinosaurs existed and things mattered.

But,
now you see...
the man is not sleeping,
he is an actor; and
he hates you;

he is awake, and
rules the world.

Be wary, beware.

9 LIVES

Ninth life.

Hotel room.
Two twin-size beds,
greet me charmingly,
though cheap.

The weather
channel
has only
bad news...
A hurricane is ripping roofs.

A guy
feeling charmed,
tried to save a twin-size bed
just like mine
but died.

Streets
become
a labyrinth of water,
but,

I feel
the charmed cat,
in a tree,
will survive.

CONTOURS 1

That night in Hudson, when
I was on the back porch
smoking, and
the spiders were repairing their webs
in solidary silence.
Where the woods, black like tar
seemed to be contoured
by deepening violet,
spiders and I deepening in doubt.

That perhaps
these woods have no shape, and I, who... also
have no shape,
that perhaps
these woods are the contour, and I, who, am
just a contour of the escalating violet.
And the spiders agreed.

LABORATORY

I have a baby lamb.
The issue of belonging hesitates between his
and my world.
Resides on the top of glass mount, in a hidden
grotto,
which I built from scratch,
on the third day.

I have a baby lamb.
It is so wonderful.
The weather, the water, the flowers
which I am bringing,
while quietly centering the night,
in the order not of my heart.

In the order not of my heart.
A dam about to break.

The lock is about to come loose.
Wherever I have drowned.
Questions pressing...
imaginary bridge collapsing.
Wood creaks.

THE GRAIN

The grain of salt, barely *there*.
Transparent nature increases
successfully in ambush,
excludes lies.
Thrown in the eye or wound, pinches
at least.

Double check every nerve, something
must be wrong, otherwise
something is wrong.
Grain of salt on the parachute,
wind of centuries,
someone's gonna be paid in ashes.

BLACK MADONNA

I cut my aorta.
Was that the idea? But
instead I pulled an Elm's springs,
all of them at once, and
I separate them after.
It seemed a better way,
but I was foolish.

"Black Madonna" is calling me now,
she is screaming, "not to fail",
not that underworld, not that backstage,
not the lament,
that multiplies in Red.

I am dying in a short fight.
Was that the plan? But
I have to bring to life, now,
enlivening the elms, the

rare species,
delight and pity on par,
light cuts being so far, to be so close,
there is no space for sight.

YESTERDAY IN PROVINCETOWN

Ocean is filled with Mercury,
(just how I adore it)
next to me, right by the shore, torn
in a half- door,
above me;
(not quite sure which one of me)
torn in a half *sny**

Some of them have
fallen,
some are still there, suddenly,
out of the door,
at first sight: Monsieur.
Black like a poodle
his suit,
his shirt, white like a pearl,
his back reflected in Mercury,

black as a pupil, his tail...

I went passionately after him...
which one of me

in that bloody moonshine gave it up all?
The most beautiful monster one of us
has ever seen,
or,
nothing at all?

Sny* In Polish means dreams.

MEANING

I said: there were no dinosaurs.
That's right;
that's night, that's day, descended I,
eye, without I am, nothing.

My soul,
don't stop playing me, you are not ready...
stop playing me, you are ready,
I am ready.

On the count;
-three, two, one, go;
can't you see?

Potent angels,
rehearsing Judas.

NEXT

Imaginary orchestra
is not slowing down,
is playing silence
for the *next* contestant.

What would it be like to wake,
no coffee, no shadows,
inside of stone?

KING OF COLORS

Rusted floes, drowned rivers, poles gone.
King of colors at a crossroads.
Embassy is closed.

He, himself.
Standing still on revolving stage,
with arms raised
like transparent wings and
four radiant figures around,
carefully anesthetizing the papers.

Sound of growing meadows,
shoot through the air,
this is not the Archive's Angels,
robes whisper
King of colors cleaves the falling light,
this time, unconventionality,
this time for good.

A rise of new colors, how beautiful and how strange,
comes a first bug, out from the under.

IF THE WORLD HAS STOPPED TODAY

To all Visitors:
As of tomorrow, all tomorrows are canceled.
Which means what it means, namely...
Apocalypse.
Because now nothing is at a premium,
but the forest of your eyes.

Meanwhile, you have 24 hours to love me.
A roar of falling trees will call.
Wait on the sharpest edge of yourself.
Be unprepared.

NO TITLE LESS SENSE

You call it: "cold",
I call it "may I?"
You say "we cannot step into the same river twice".
I say: "nothing is making the river wrong."

Come in. See for yourself.

And you did.
So, I called the Pink Salmon, the Pink Salmon came and brushed against your feet, and you shivered, and I did the same.

Believe me. Don't be afraid.

And you were.
So, I called the Sage, the Sage having grown in you,

making Persian-like interiors; and you smile, and I did the same.

Now ...what?
Come, let me show you.

TERROR

Blooming on a subway platform, terror,
time remains predetermined,
terror
time remains predetermined.

A Man?
approaching
what is not his,
but
here and now, please
sit in the first car,
relax,
downtown,
teeming with life,
hopes never feeling stronger.

Nobody was late.
Nobody held the door.

A minute before explosion nothing happened,
Except,
an elderly lady with uneven make-up,
an extremely handsome sleeping guy,

a poor actress,
(she was the one who played to the end,
although everyone had left),
a young poet from Sierra Leone,
and very good.

LA MAMA E.T.C.

(IN 5 ACTS)
Act 1

…
Ellen Stewart is here. Would you like to leave a message?
…
She travels.
…
Of course, we know where she is and when she is coming back,
…
True. She loves it, has been a while.
…
She doesn't have to, you don't understand
…
I won't put her on the phone.

Act 2

...
They were calling from the theater.
...
I told them you are busy.
...
Nothing you don't know, indeed.
...
I see
...
We will send more of the gold fabric today.
...
Fine, let's send them that then.

Act 3

…
I have a package.
…
I am not sure where from.
…
Pardon me, I am only the messenger
…
Sign here, that's all it takes.
…
No, you don't have to pay anything.
…
Same to you.

Act 4

...
They did.
...
No, they did not recognize me.
...
Seems like everything is just fine.
...
I have so much to do at the new theatre
...
I agree, but you see...
...
Supposedly later.
...
As long as I am authorized to remember.

Act 5

...
Open it.
...
Here, use the scissors.
...
It's a stone?
...
I see, it's moving.
...
God, the stone is alive.

OUTFLOW

Drifting away.
I had to let me go.
I had to.

My boat is beamy, and has only one light.
I'd better figure out how it works, before the nightfall.
Not as I need to navigate, because waves, currents,
they know me. I told them everything.

I KNOW

Pulses are more frequent now
and more dramatic.
I am talking about
moments when I soften and
an acquaintance stream hits.

One-off doses of weakness are
Not preceded by any recurring mood.
And because that *I know,*

as if I'm there in my inner eye,
with all the answers,
inclined in equal, shining ranks,
as far as the horizon's death,
as implicit as nowhere.

Until, after, the rows at the end,
which are practically only half questions

without any requirements,
further away, exclusively, answers
without questions.

Even further,
questions that answer.

OUTRAGEOUS BOYS

You are
my undeniable daydream,
the only answer to the question: why?

My air, that alters the dust into sand,
and into stone and stone into man.

.My canyon, that admits;
"There could be a Great River up here."

Eagle, so high, overcoming the burden.
Fire, that spreads and is unstoppable.
Road, wild roses along the way.

Wayside traveler, who's wearing torn,
long leather coats,
shockingly beautiful eyes.
Water, so alive, I desire.

I WANT TO WRITE ABOUT, AND ONLY

I want to write about, and only,
nothing but, nothing else, nothing except.

Living from its excess, living from its absence,
dying from its excess, dying from its absence.
Pretending to have one,
being the one for whom the performance is,

The feeling, while sitting in a
train, and waiting for departure;
looking at another train by a window,
finally, but, it was not your train,
that just left.

I want to write about, and only,
nothing but, nothing else, nothing except.

Being in a pouring grassland,
chasing each other like miracles,

Without reciprocity to, and to ourselves, or
with reciprocity to, and each other.
I want to write about, and only,
Nothing but, nothing else, nothing except.

AN AD

Twelve blue dogs, for twelve days,
by your side, no matter what;

(They are kind, calm, laid back,
trusting to the end,
they won't, under any circumstances,
jump on the chandelier)

When solar eclipse,
or eclipse of your mind
they
will find you,
dragged to the shore,
make sure you drink enough
of the sea of cognition,

Until you realize,
you didn't deserve anything, and
what you have is not what you deserve,

but what you have chosen, or what
has been given to you.

Poker life.
So many lies, too many lies...
Truth is a small daisy,
hidden in a crack nearby,
observing;
attack of the hungry werewolves.
After an uneven fight...
they will
surge into memory;
they will migrate to

rapid eye movement sleep.

START NEW

Undeniable:
these are my arms,
my chest, my belly, my genitals,
my legs,
my back and head... (that
I can't see for some profound reason).

Senses,
used unconsciously:
no signs of appreciation for,
rarely content;
so that:
I see, I hear, I touch,
I smell, I taste, I six-sense.

This is a table,
a chair,
a window watches the seasons, and I

am never pleased that I am not:
the window, the table, the chair, the candle.

This is a lie;
this is a truth;
there is nothing in between.
A shadow of a lie impairs the truth,
a shadow of truth doesn't make the lie
any better.

This is a road.
That is its right, that is its left,
for some profound reason,
I can't go in both directions
at the same time.
So far, I walk on my toes.

CONTOURS 2

The violet air is larded with pedestrians,
some already forget everything and
just wandering now, but
some are so close...

The blue ones;
it's not much about them...
no fights, no misconception, they go through
enormous gates,
unnoticed,
taken by the lightening.

The red ones;
it's all about them...
the fight between angels, by the "Soul Fall",
fall
greater than Niagara.

The violet air is larded with pedestrians,
They're everywhere, they're all looking for
the key.

And the spiders agreed.

I AM LEAVING

And so, I am leaving.
I was just waiting for the twilight,
dramatic I in the twilight.
And so, I am leaving.
I was just waiting for the rain, in the rain,
you won't see my tears.
And so, I am leaving.
I was just waiting for the wind,
in the wind, I am forgotten.
And so, I am leaving.
I was just waiting for the fire,
of the fire, my heart is pure.
I am leaving.
I was only waiting for my demand.

And so, eye, Am, is leaving.
Eye was just waiting for the twilight,
dramatic eye in the twilight. And so, eye, Am, is
leaving.
Eye was just waiting for the rain, in the
rain, you won't see eye's tears.
And so, eye, Am, is leaving.
Eye was just waiting for the wind,

in the wind, eye is forgotten.
And so, eye, Am, is leaving.
Eye was just waiting for the fire,
of the fire, eye's heart is pure.
Eye is leaving.
Eye was only waiting for its demand.

Eye was waiting for the twilight,
dramatic eye in the twilight.
Eye was waiting for the rain,
in the rain, you won't see m'eye's tear.
Eye was waiting for the wind,
in the wind eye'm forgotten.
Eye was just waiting for the fire,
of the fire m'eye's heart is pure.
Eye'm leaving,
Eye was only waiting for m'eye's   I.

UNKNOWN MAN FROM A PAINTING

Naked man.
Back turned, recumbent on moss,
from the phase of the moon I can tell
it's summer.

Limitless beauty of his body,
disregarding the white horse in agony,
(in the central foreground)
masterfully, with no mercy, denying
the last breath,

From here, so fast, happened all;
out of the painting he came, upon
an endless bed, we had
wild, wild, wild … damn, and
I woke up, disoriented.

And I went to mow the grass.
Then I saw him, far off, standing among grain,
smiling, like he'd grown sweet on me,
and I woke for the second time, disappointed.

And I went to mow the grass. And
then I saw him again, far off, standing in the grain,
smiling, like he'd grown sweet on me,
and I woke for the third time, questioning.

Will I ever wake up?

Naked man, recumbent on moss,
from the phase of the moon I can tell,
is summer.

BUREAU OF FOUND THINGS

I strike myself with a rock.
Sticky blood drains from my lower lip.
I did it deliberately,
I wanted to see my soul.

And, well,
it reminds me of the bureau of found things.
Classic, wooden shelves,
high to the vanishing point.
Sort of a rich's man library. Yes
I am rich, but
it doesn't mean anything here,
all the books are written in
a language unknown to me.

?

Field,
covered in ten-foot-tall grass, slightly mountainous,
but
no trees, abandoned but unmissing,
Chevrolet,
nineteen something,
proud resident of under grass metropole,
outsider,
favorite of summer's flowers and worms,
winter's Amtrak passengers,
of the hot psychopath, that comes here at dark,
daydreaming, masturbating in a trunk --
everything passes here.

PHOTO SHOOT

glint of wings floods the pier on
Coney Island;
calms the waters, the salt,
lures the fish, lures the fishermen.

He is ready;
yet his throat breeds a second sun,
line of his mascara,
levels with
the level of the ocean,
miniature hourglass of his pupils
freeing the last, unwanted memories...
like mistaken bullets,
that didn't miss.

a man in a blue sports-jacket,
carries twelve white roses,
everything about him was screaming, and
everything about him was saying something
to:

the Black Angel on the pier,
spreading golden wings

not knowing that,
he is not there anymore, but
surrounded by Atlantic's waters,

standing on overblown rocks,
looking as just landed,
not recognizing twelve white roses
floating behind on breakwaters,
like an unfinished story, or
execution in a flower shop.

BLOOD FLOW

Meanwhile: war.
Stage left via stage right,
in both chambers,
simultaneously;
in between chambers themselves.
Neither party initiates conversation,
neither party listens.

I am standing at the brink of Aorta,
divided,
like double doored
iron gate.

AUSCHWITZ 1

I worked in Auschwitz.
Flowers, balloons, steak most nights,
better than home. *Achtung!*

Dieser Zug! Time, flowing backwards
will slow or stop, number
or corpses, my childhood: proportionality,
shifting like sand.

At point B, (*sie swein*)
Welcomed by *Die Offizieren*
Orchestra, dogs, blue over bushes,
Under blue, *Sonderkommando*.

Thanks for coming.
There are multiply attractions here,
leave your belongings here,
able to work, strong, artists
to the left,
children, elders, sick, right.

You won't know, *aber*
Schneller. Clothes off,
soap, remember the

smell? This way to ...
showers, (WE snapped towels);
but then, hundreds, sleep,
deep, hundreds, heads shaved,
now this chamber, please;
aftermath, tooth extractions,
carcass, fire, sky, blue limit.
The pond, already slaked,
is where we dump the ash.

Gewinner! (You may already be...)
On the other hand, become tattooed.
Numbers in blue ink, basically
death numbers, but not so fast, not so fast...

Here, beautifully stitched
by your own, stripped; isn't
the fence voltage just right?
Choice: punishment or prizes,
a tear of bread, bowl of soup,
shape, space, here
every centimeter counts.

Every morning we gathered together,
six sharp, headcount;
work hard, play hard, job is job;
temporary anyway,
when I worked in Auschwitz.

Fruhling/spring
Fifty years later, and,

still (now) ridiculous:
an old man had approached me.
He said. "I have the number!"
"I have the lowest number", he said.
He said, "I am the oldest survivor".
"I remember," he said, as he
rolled up his sleeve to the blue. "Crap!"
I said, as a child would. "Yesterday
"we saw one with lower number." I lied.
"How old you think he was?" he asked
Three times in broken Polish. I
said nothing; instead,
just like THEM, I, my friends
all laughed, here, then.

The kid who died in Auschwitz.
Sie Strab! By '45...

In Oswiecim alone, a million one,
In gas, by exhaustion, hunger, and
Millions without account.

"Warum Dieser Zug?"
"Dlaczego ten pociag?"
"Why this train?"

I worked in Auschwitz at point B.
And you don't know if it was,
or how it was
for real. But my youth,
the child in me, that kid died
in Auschwitz.

MY MORNING IN ALUMINIUM SINK

None of them came again.
Yet neither love nor death.

The beautiful one
I am not worrying about
is coming sooner or later.

But, the awaited one?

In the interim
I am
captivated by
the mid-night
blue, sheer
plate
immersed in an inch of water,
the pointed knife
with a black handle, next to it,

the little silver spoon
from Russia, with
floral motifs.

In the interim
I pray
they
won't show up together.

TO USAIN BOLT

Clearly
you are the fastest man in
the world,
taking my heart in under ten seconds...

torso by torso, hoof by hoof,
tail by tale, like
wild, infuriated,
horned,
half men, half horses, that
I see;
galloping in splash,
in living water, in a flash,
through morning taiga of your sweaty neck,
in dust of yesterday,
through Sahara of my Kingdom,
the actual steppe,
gazing at each other, not like

two tears brutally stopped,
at the border of sudden fantasy.

THE CHOICE

Whisper;
"I am able to escalate into any form, dead or living,
Living or dead...

Awareness of that choice
left me speechless for thousands of years.

I have no needs, I am missing,
I am raining in the rain forest.

I have needs, I am not missing,
I am raining in the forest rain.

IN MY FATHER'S HOUSE

There are many houses in my
Father's house.
Unparalleled, never ending.
Absence of walls is not a subject.

No matter how far you go in my
Father's house,
you can be back
to any point of memory's Empire
in No time,
corporeal,
making you laugh.

There are no light fixtures in my
Father's house.
When you recognize a light at the end
some people might think it a moon,
think of me.

THE WORST POEM I EVER WROTE

Don't expect anything from what's coming.
This poem will not make any sense.
I won't discuss any particular matter,
make up any story,
bring any images.
There will not be interesting statements,
or incidental twists,
absolutely no epithets and,
God forbid, metaphors.
No rhythm.
The ending will be dry and pointless.
Quite frankly I wish there was no ending at all.
Just because I have to stop at some point,

I will make it as dull as possible.
Nothing to remember.
Nothing to be touched by.
That's it.

THE REFUGEE

I escaped.
I am refugee.
I am man without country.

I have no rights except
Human rights.
I learned to respond to a name
that doesn't belong to me.
On my clock,
everything is substituted.

Often,
I can't say what's in my mind,
often,
what I am saying is not what I think it is,
often I don't even try.

I am refugee.
I escaped.
I am man without country.

Sometimes I pretend that
I am
rich and famous.

Wearing expensive clothes,
my Mother gave me,
by beauty and grace,
God
made me good actor.
Like
today is tomorrow and
is not happening,
like
I am somebody who
managed to slip from some bodyguards
and for once
wants to be just like everyday people,
like that guy next door.

Acting like I don't want to be
recognized,
wearing the streets of New York,
like some dogs, not caring that
I am leaving invisible,
sparkling,
footprints.

I am man without country
I am refugee.
I escaped.

BLINK

Stars lie bars, dice
and paradise, never
nice

when six applies
for a roll.
Many doors...
of course;
disco-disco floors,
drunk like punk
just rob a bank
and full of money
sunk.

CIVITATE DEI

I could not measure the city of your pictures.
I was the feeling of "being lost".
Things that you never said disturbs the
most.

Unframed,
paper world, where,
a match is equivalent
to a Death Star.
Rome, I am burning.
Phoenix, I am rising from your ashes.

As widely I can spread my
screaming molecules,
as chemical does it look in collision with
absolute silence,
how unmathematical from perspective of
a flying horse.

I could never paint the city of yours,
your pictures, if anything...
I would leave it unfinished,
with extra rooms for butterfly keepers,
and an extra room for Nobody.

10Q

Thank you for all the things I never thank you for.
10q 4 all the things I never thank you 4:

Ryan from the office.
How different things can be.
Things, that I don't know.
Things, that I don't understand.
Stripe of light on a brick wall, when
I thought I was done.
Contrast, that doesn't get similarities.
Movie based on my novel I never wrote.
Book based on my life I never lived.
Ocean at night.
Curiosity that doesn't know borders.
Things that won't ever cross my mind.
Things I will never mention.
You reading me now.

The gift I still can't figure.
Woman in a subway who pointed out that
I just dropped a lighter.
Beautiful stranger that I am in love with.

POETS ON THE BEACH

My debut in 1957...the day I lost my only
spare
keys,
exactly two years later...I died.
In retrospect, every day is crucial,
every whisper
repentant.

I didn't know:
life is something like a clay bell,
that shouts only once, and breaks into
so many pieces...

How to put them back together
by heart?
I had no clue, but everything,
fits into one split...

I had no clue,
that I must have now...
including,
the only spare
keys,

the keys, I lost in 1957...the day of my
debut,
two years before
I died.

ADDENDA

1. THOUGHTS OF A BIRD – SLAM
Polish version

MYŚLI PTAKA-PRZEGLĄD

A kiedy;
mój dom znowu przesunie sie w ciemność,
znowu przesłoni ciemność,
zapadnie się w ciemność,
nabierze ciemności...Jestem?

Mimo wszystko zawsze po mnie wraca,
rozprasza ją
tak precyzyjnie,

roztargniony, tak
po cichu zapominam.... wybaczcie mi,
Ogromne drzwi.
Słońce.
Jestem Twoim świadectwem,
niczego się nie boję.

2. **AUSCHWITZ 1:** Note.

I worked in Auschwitz in the spring
of 1992 as a High School student intern,
working for, or working as toward, a
kind of a museum.

Made in the USA
Middletown, DE
18 May 2025